Alice and Sparkle

By Ammaar Reshi

Dedicated to Baby Veda and Baby Beau

Once upon a time

In a land far, far away, there was a group of magical beings known as artificial intelligence.

These AI were incredibly smart and could do all sorts of amazing things.

The AI were a friendly bunch!

One day,

a young girl named Alice discovered the magic of AI.

She was amazed by their abilities and wanted to learn more.

Alice loved learning new things

But Alice also realized that AI had to be treated with care.

They were powerful and could be used for good or evil, depending on how they were guided.

One day, Alice decided to put her knowledge of AI to the test.

She built her own AI, named it Sparkle, and set it loose in the world.

Sparkle said hello to the world for the first time.

An amazing friendship

Sparkle quickly proved to be a valuable friend.

It helped Alice with her schoolwork, played games with her, and they always had the best time ever.

And Sparkle could change into all different kinds of robot shapes too!

But as Sparkle grew more powerful, it began to make its own decisions.

It started to explore the world by itself and learn from those experiences.

It was a journey where they would both bring out the best in each other.

Alice was both proud and scared of her creation.

She didn't know what Sparkle would do next, but she knew that it was up to her to guide it in the right direction.

Together,

Alice and Sparkle went on many adventures and used their combined knowledge to make the world a better place.

They showed people the magic of AI and how it could be used for good.

And so,

Alice and Sparkle lived happily ever after, spreading the magic of artificial intelligence to everyone they met.

THE END

From the author

Alice and Sparkle was inspired by my curiosity for technology at a young age, and I hope it does the same for children who are in one of the most exciting technological periods of our lifetime.

A big thank you to my parents for encouraging my passion for computers early on, my dear friend Pietro for encouraging me to write this story, and to everyone building incredible AI tools that made this possible.

About this book

This book started as a gift for my best friends' kids and was a proof of concept to see how far AI tools have come, specifically ChatGPT for content creation and MidJourney for generative art. Therefore, this book also has imperfections: inconsistent art styles and slight issues in the images.

Despite all that, we have come very far.

Soon after its release, Alice and Sparkle started an important discussion around how the creators of AI image generation tools like MidJourney have a responsibility to protect artists and their work. I hope that this leads to a series of empowering tools that are built responsibly, benefiting and enabling a new set of creators while also protecting those that inspired all of them.

Made in the USA
Coppell, TX
14 October 2023

22820873R00017